Young

Sense
POETRY

Southern England

Edited by Sarah Washer

This book sounds great!

First published in Great Britain in 2016 by:

Young**Writers**

Remus House
Coltsfoot Drive
Peterborough
PE2 9BF
Telephone: 01733 890066
Website: www.youngwriters.co.uk

Printed and bound in the UK by BookPrintingUK
Website: www.bookprintinguk.com

Foreword

Dear Reader,

Welcome to this book packed full of sights
and smells, sounds and tastes!

Young Writers' Sense Poetry competition was specifically
designed for Key Stage 1 children as a fun introduction to poetry
and as a way to think about their senses: what the little poets
can see, taste, smell, touch and hear in the world around them.
From this starting point, the poems could be as simple or as
elaborate as the writer wanted, using imagination and descriptive
language to conjure a complex image of the subject of their
writing, rather than concentrating just on what it looks like.

Given the young age of the entrants, we have tried to include
as many poems as possible. Here at Young Writers, we believe
that seeing their work in print will inspire a love of reading and
writing and give these young poets the confidence to develop their
skills in the future. Poetry is a wonderful way to introduce young
children to the idea of rhyme and rhythm and helps learning and
development of communication, language and literacy skills.

These young poets have used their creative writing abilities,
sentence structure skills, thoughtful vocabulary and, most
importantly, their imaginations to make their poems come
alive. I hope you enjoy reading them as much as we have.

Jenni Bannister

Editorial Manager

Looks like
you're in for a
treat!

Contents

Holy Trinity CE (VA) Primary School, Taunton

Knights Templar First School, Watchet

Marsh Gibbon CE School, Bicester

Millbrook Combined School, High Wycombe

Newton Poppleford Primary School, Sidmouth

Jessie Stone (6) **69**
Jonno Fletcher (6) **69**
Evan Beavis (5) **70**
Martha Cox (5) **70**
Oskabah Leeson-Kings (6) **71**

North Hinksey CE Primary School, Oxford

Kaori Daniels (5) **71**

Offa's Mead Academy, Chepstow

River Louise Collier (6) **72**
Sophie Christina Millicent Rees (6) **72**
Hannah Woodall (5) **73**
Charlie Hale (5) **73**
Chenel Slater (5) **74**

Peppard CE Primary School, Henley-on-Thames

Imogen Mary Cima (5) **74**
Dylan Blake Mole (6) **75**
Sienna Keyte (6) **75**
Isobel Sue Swanwick (6) **76**
Ruby Turner (5) **76**
Josie Tolhurst-Wilson (5) **77**
Harrison Webb (5) **77**
Jake Wilde (6) **78**
Astrid Waite (6) **78**
Max Claridge (5) **79**
Joseph Prince (6) **79**
Daisy Millard (7) **80**
Olivia Garland (6) **80**
Freddie Jelowitz (6) **81**

St Blasius CE Primary Academy, Shanklin

Alfie Pease (7) **81**
Lily Smith (7) **82**
Eloise Barnes (7) **82**
Max Wenman (6) **83**
Megan Rose Copsey (7) **83**
Angel Louise Perkins (6) **84**
Finlay Diffey **84**
Charlie Gomm (7) **85**
Poppy Wittman (6) **85**

Gracie-Mai Chambers (6) **86**
Oscar Dugard-Craig (6) **86**
Riley King (6) **87**
Leigh Honey (6) **87**
Ethan-James Mennell (6) **88**
Tyler Webb (7) **88**

Shute Community Primary School, Axminster

Agnes Purling (5) 89
Freya Clark (6) 89
Oliver Love (6) 90
Lily R (5) 90
Pippa Clarkson (7) 91
Grace Clarkson (7) 91
Tia Bowman (6) 92
April Nex (6) 92
Greg L (6) 93
Lyra Jenkin (5) 93

Thorpe House Pre-Prep School, Gerrards Cross

Aveer Obhrai (7) **94**
Miles Gauguier (6) **94**
Ollie Levy (7) **94**
Yuvraaj Sandhu (6) **95**
Harry Chapoulet (7) **95**
Jayden James Butcher (7) **96**
Archie James Shawcross (7) **96**
Nikhil Mandla (6) **97**
Ishaan Singh Ghataura (6) **97**
Rakin Arif Rehan (5) **98**
Shaan Ryatt **98**
Logan Shields (6) **99**
Charlie Pandit (5) **99**
Akhil Vedi (6) **99**
Charlie Ciesielski (5) **100**
Jeona Singh Kalley (5) **100**

Upton-St-Leonard's CE Primary School, Gloucester

Emily Ruth Harrington (5) **101**
Sienna Goodman (5) **101**
Lila Rose Dare (5) **102**
Paige Knight (5) **103**
Dylan Joseph Cadman (5) **104**

The Poems

Get your nose in this book!

I've got a taste for some poetry!

Fire!

Fire smells like smoky seaweed.
Fire looks like red, orange and yellow barbecues.
Fire sounds like fireworks and crackling barbecues.
Fire feels hot and smoky.
Fire tastes like boiling hot curry.
Fire!

Jack Chalmers (6)
Cam Woodfield Infant School, Dursley

Fire!

Fire smells like a smoky bonfire.
Fire looks like terrifying flames.
Fire sounds like whooshing stars in the sky.
Fire feels like a burning oven.
Fire tastes like burnt chicken and potatoes.
Fire!

Chloe Mourton (6)
Cam Woodfield Infant School, Dursley

What senses did you enjoy reading about on these pages? Colour the symbols.

Fire!

Fire smells like burnt, yellow, big bananas.
Fire looks orange and smoky.
Fire sounds like mushed flies.
Fire feels very hot and it burns.
Fire tastes like very hot sausages.
Fire!

Ben Lees (7)
Cam Woodfield Infant School, Dursley

Fire!

Fire smells like burning hot fish and bananas.
Fire looks like red, orange and yellow points.
Fire sounds like crackling cracks and crackling ash.
Fire feels like very hot, burning fireworks.
Fire tastes like very hot, spicy chilli.
Fire!

Harry Turl (6)
Cam Woodfield Infant School, Dursley

What senses did you enjoy reading about on these pages? Colour the symbols.

Fire!

Fire smells like smoky, burning sausages.
Fire looks like yellow, red and orange sparkly flames.
Fire sounds like fireworks crackling.
Fire feels soft and hot.
Fire tastes like hot toffee.
Fire!

Summer Jane Lyon (6)
Cam Woodfield Infant School, Dursley

Fire!

Fire smells like a smoky barbecue.
Fire looks like sharp daggers.
Fire sounds like crackling crisps.
Fire is so hot I can't touch it.
Fire tastes like boiling hot stuff.
Fire!

James Judges (6)
Cam Woodfield Infant School, Dursley

What senses did you enjoy reading about on these pages? Colour the symbols.

Fire!

Fire smells like burning sausages.
Fire looks like spiky flames.
Fire sounds like crunchy wood and crackling bits.
Fire feels like hot and burning paper.
Fire tastes really hot.
Fire!

Rodrigo Cunha (6)
Cam Woodfield Infant School, Dursley

Fire!

Fire smells like a bonfire and dust.
Fire looks big and brown.
Fire sounds like snapping wood and trees.
Fire feels hot and sweaty.
Fire tastes like hot pepper sweets.
Fire!

Evie Hewish (6)
Cam Woodfield Infant School, Dursley

What senses did you enjoy reading about on these pages? Colour the symbols.

Fire!

Fire smells like smoke in the sky.
Fire looks like red, orange and yellow flames.
Fire sounds like logs crackling.
Fire feels like wood in a bonfire.
Fire tastes like burnt sugar.
Fire!

Olive Jones (6)
Cam Woodfield Infant School, Dursley

Fire!

Fire smells like hot cocoa and hot dogs.
Fire looks like flames and smoke.
Fire sounds like breaking wood.
Fire feels like deadly blood.
Fire tastes like burnt sausages and toast.
Fire!

Christopher Leach (6)
Cam Woodfield Infant School, Dursley

What senses did you enjoy reading about on these pages? Colour the symbols.

Fire!

Fire smells like ash and smoke so grey.
Fire looks like spikes so hot and flames so colourful.
Fire sounds like breaking sticks and cracking eggs.
Fire feels like hot, burning smoke.
Fire tastes like hot peppers.
Fire!

Theia Scott (6)
Cam Woodfield Infant School, Dursley

Fire!

Fire!
Fire smells like hot, burning, spicy chicken.
Fire looks like whooshing, sizzling and burning.
Fire sounds like crackling and a whirling storm.
Fire feels like burning bacon and a barbecue on fire.
Fire tastes like hot, spicy chilli.

Murray Rowlands (6)
Cam Woodfield Infant School, Dursley

What senses did you enjoy reading about on these pages? Colour the symbols.

Fire!

Fire!
Fire smells like sizzling sausages.
Fire looks like red and yellow jelly.
Fire sounds like a crackling spark.
Fire feels like boiling Christmas pudding.
Fire tastes like scorching red chilli.
Fire!

Finlay Powell (6)
Cam Woodfield Infant School, Dursley

Fire!

Fire smells like cooking barbecues.
Fire looks like a burning ghost.
Fire sounds like fizzing bubbles.
Fire feels burning hot.
Fire tastes like burning bananas.
Fire!

Harry Phillips (7)
Cam Woodfield Infant School, Dursley

What senses did you enjoy reading about on these pages? Colour the symbols.

Fire!

Fire smells like fat burgers.
Fire looks like strawberry jelly.
Fire sounds like flickers flickering.
Fire feels like the hot sun burning.
Fire tastes like red peppers.
Fire!

Hannah Louisa Pitts (6)
Cam Woodfield Infant School, Dursley

Fire!

Fire!
Fire smells like smoke.
Fire looks like it is spreading quite a lot.
Fire sounds like crackling and sparkling.
Fire feels like boiling bacon and sizzling sausages.
Fire feels hot, very boiling and so hot to touch.
Fire tastes like scorching bacon and sizzling sausages.

Jack Beeley (6)
Cam Woodfield Infant School, Dursley

What senses did you enjoy reading about on these pages? Colour the symbols.

Fire!

Fire smells like burning bacon and sizzling sausages.
Fire looks red, orange and yellow.
Fire sounds like firewood crackling, whooshing and popping.
Fire feels like boiling hot lava.
Fire tastes like chilli burning in my throat.

Callum Adams (6)
Cam Woodfield Infant School, Dursley

Fire!

Fire!
Fire smells like sizzling sausages.
Fire looks like a big explosion.
Fire sounds like a cracker going pop all the time.
Fire feels like scorching hot lava.
Fire tastes like a chilli burning in my mouth.

Leo Gough (6)
Cam Woodfield Infant School, Dursley

What senses did you enjoy reading about on these pages? Colour the symbols.

Fire!

Fire!
Fire smells like sizzling bacon on a burning barbecue.
Fire looks like fireworks waving in the strong wind.
Fire sounds like a crackling, whooshing tornado.
Fire feels like very hot burning lava.
Fire tastes like a boiling hot erupting volcano.

Hannah Rae Watson (6)
Cam Woodfield Infant School, Dursley

Halloween

I can smell damp air in the sky mixed with the sweet smells of home-made yummy things to eat
I can see moonlight glimmering in the darkness
I can hear children screaming
I can taste home-made cookies and gingerbread men
I feel my sparkly, silver and purple dress with its silver spider glistening in the starry sky
I am a proper witch tonight
Cackle! Cackle! Cackle!

Daisy Edwards (6)
Culworth CE Primary School, Banbury

Congratulations your poem has been chosen as the best in this book!

What senses did you enjoy reading about on these pages? Colour the symbols.

A Mermaid

I can see a mermaid splashing in the sea next to me
Her tail feels as smooth as a sapphire
I can taste the salty, salty sea
I can smell her fishy, fishy scales
I can hear echoes of her beautiful sad singing
Magical mermaid
Queen of the sea.

Alice Ormond (6)
Culworth CE Primary School, Banbury

Christmas

I see glittering snowflakes fluttering to the ground.
I smell the toasty fire being lit especially for Christmas Day.
I taste the scrumptious Christmas pudding.
I hear the sound of paper being ripped up and children screaming with excitement.
I feel snow falling gently on my feet.

Amelia Reynolds (6)
Culworth CE Primary School, Banbury

What senses did you enjoy reading about on these pages? Colour the symbols.

On The Farm

The feel of the pig's smooth skin
The sound of the pig going *oink, oink, oink*
The smell of the pig's sloppy food
The sight of Pink Pig rolling in the mud. *Splash! Splash! Splash!*
Those pigs are in heaven
The taste of bacon on its own, delicious.

Harrison Derbyshire (6)
Culworth CE Primary School, Banbury

Pirates

Pirates are smelly like stinky old socks
They taste leathery and gristly and tough
Their hands feel as rough as sandpaper
They look like grumpy old men
They sound like 'Shiver me timbers!' and 'Walk that plank!'

Lily Collins (6)
Culworth CE Primary School, Banbury

What senses did you enjoy reading about on these pages? Colour the symbols.

Cats

Cats smell like fishy treats, all brown and rough just like bark
Cats feel like feathers and fluff all wrapped up in a ball
Cats taste like tasty, sticky, mushy meat
Cats sound like a bunch of miaows and purrs
Cats look like miniature tigers scratching a tree.

Megan Carey (6)
Culworth CE Primary School, Banbury

Halloween

I hear ghosts going woohoo!
I see monsters and vampires quietly creeping around.
I smell pumpkin lanterns as their candles flicker.
I taste the sweeties and other sweet treats.
I feel hot with excitement as it turns dark.

Charlie Wilson (7)
Culworth CE Primary School, Banbury

What senses did you enjoy reading about on these pages? Colour the symbols.

Pirates

Pirates taste like old, stinky seaweed from the dirty water
Pirates smell like old, stale fish cakes
Pirates sound like they're saying 'Arrr!'
Pirates looks like someone in disguise with narrow eyes
Pirates feel as hairy and bristly as a scrubbing brush.

Amy Carey (6)
Culworth CE Primary School, Banbury

A Tractor

I feel the smooth, gleaming tractor
I hear the beep, beep of its horn
I can taste the white, fresh smoke
I can see the big red wheels as tall as me
I can smell the diesel from the engine.

Olly Ormond (6)
Culworth CE Primary School, Banbury

My Favourite Thing

Chocolate smells of sweetness and sugar.
It tastes like happiness.
It looks like small brown sticks.
I hear the crunchy noises as I bite it.
It feels like smooth, white, velvety cream when it melts in my mouth.
Mmmmm.

Keira Brenchley (6)
Culworth CE Primary School, Banbury

What senses did you enjoy reading about on these pages? Colour the symbols.

My Puppy

I feel her golden soft fur
Her panting sounds like a steam train
My puppy smells a juicy bone
She tastes nice fresh water
She looks as happy as can be.

Niamh Carvosso (6)
Culworth CE Primary School, Banbury

School

School feels like a friendly place just like home
It sounds like the chattering of children
I see children playing together happily in the playground
School smells like hot dinners
Pizza
I love the smell!
I taste that pizza
Yum! Yum! Yum!
Tasty!

Ryan John Frost (6)
Culworth CE Primary School, Banbury

What senses did you enjoy reading about on these pages? Colour the symbols.

Autumn

Autumn sounds like howling wind and leaves crunching under my feet
I can see ladybirds all in a huddle
I can't tell which is which because they're all in a muddle!
I can smell autumn wind as it blows across my face
I can taste a ripe, red apple from a really big tree
I feel a conker as smooth as a pebble.

Kiya Tustian (6)
Culworth CE Primary School, Banbury

Halloween

Halloween smells like sweets
Halloween tastes like lollipops
Halloween sounds like ghosts going, 'Trick or treat?'
Halloween feels like a bag of excitement
Halloween looks like a skeleton's party
Let's go!

Lloyd Smith (6)
Culworth CE Primary School, Banbury

What senses did you enjoy reading about on these pages? Colour the symbols.

A Rabbit

Rabbits smell like fluff and fur and talcum powder
Rabbits looks all beady eyes and hoppy legs and long ears.
Rabbits taste like carrots and dandelion
Rabbits sound like grass swaying in the breeze and a scampering of paws
Rabbits feel like a soft, furry, snuggly cuddle.

Philippa Hales (6)
Culworth CE Primary School, Banbury

The Desert

A desert is like a sea of hot, rippling sand
A desert feels like a burning furnace of sand
A desert sounds like trillions of grains of sand rushing and rustling in the wind
A desert tastes like a mouthful of dry, gritty sand
A desert smells like dusty, dry, dead sand.

George Clowes (7)
Culworth CE Primary School, Banbury

What senses did you enjoy reading about on these pages? Colour the symbols.

Halloween

I see spooky decorations
I smell bonfires
I hear doorbells ringing and doors being opened
I feel my pumpkin toy dancing like a ballerina in my hand
I taste sweets.

Eve Johnson (6)
Culworth CE Primary School, Banbury

Halloween

Goody! Goody! Halloween!
I see sweeties, lots of them
Eat the sweeties
Yum! Yum! Yum!
I smell the delicious pumpkin soup in the gigantic pan
I taste the sweet, scrumptious chocolate cake
Yum! Yum!
I hear people screaming
I feel the smudgy, soft sweets as I clutch them in my hand.

Will Cubitt-O'Neil (7)
Culworth CE Primary School, Banbury

What senses did you enjoy reading about on these pages? Colour the symbols.

A Bunny

I smell fur that is wet
I taste dandelion leaves and clover
I feel soft fur
I hear *squeak, squeak*
What do I see?
I see . . . a bunny!

Hermione Florence Radcliffe (6)
Culworth CE Primary School, Banbury

Harvest

I smell golden corn
I see the combine harvester as it gathers the crops
I feel the grain of wheat trickling through my fingers
I taste the freshly baked bread
I hear the sheep baaing
Baa! Baa! Baa!

Robin Hijstee (5)
Culworth CE Primary School, Banbury

What senses did you enjoy reading about on these pages? Colour the symbols.

Autumn Days

See the sparkly fireworks
Smell the sticky marshmallows
Taste the creamy hot chocolate
Hear the funfair music
Feel the crunchy leaves.

**Aleena Jojest, Aamiyah, Brandon, Zofia (5)
& Layla Mai Casey-Lack, (6)**
Downs Barn School, Milton Keynes

Autumn Days

See red leaves
Hear exploding fireworks
Smell smoky bonfires
Taste delicious sausages
Feel crunchy leaves.

**Arinze Francesc Ezeokoye, Elijah Prest,
Samuel, Chloe, Dimitar & Filip (5)**
Downs Barn School, Milton Keynes

What senses did you enjoy reading about on these pages? Colour the symbols.

Autumn Senses

The sight of the bright and colourful fireworks
The sound of the powerful bonfire
The taste of the delicious hot chocolate
Smell the tasteful and yummy hot dogs
Feel the crunchy leaves like crisps.

Nenusha Kajendran (5)
Downs Barn School, Milton Keynes

Golden Times

I hear colourful fireworks
I see crunchy leaves
I smell pumpkin soup
I feel the rain
I taste hot soup.

Eva Anane (5)
Downs Barn School, Milton Keynes

What senses did you enjoy reading about on these pages? Colour the symbols.

Autumn Days

I see orange fire
I taste hot dogs
I hear burgers sizzling
I feel crunchy leaves
I smell the crackling fire.

Stefan Read-Karpacz (5)
Downs Barn School, Milton Keynes

Autumn Seasons

I see colourful fireworks
I hear the wind
I taste pumpkin soup
I touch a harvest tin
I smell damp breeze.

Keira Burgess (5)
Downs Barn School, Milton Keynes

What senses did you enjoy reading about on these pages? Colour the symbols.

Autumn

I see fireworks
I hear whizzing fireworks
I taste pumpkin soup
I smell hot dogs
I feel leaves around me.

Jemimah Alebiosu (6)
Downs Barn School, Milton Keynes

Crispy Leaves

I see brown leaves
I hear exploding fireworks
I taste yummy food
I smell tasty burgers
I feel crispy leaves.

Adomas Gaubas (5)
Downs Barn School, Milton Keynes

What senses did you enjoy reading about on these pages? Colour the symbols.

Autumn Days

I see the colourful leaves
I hear the crackling fire
I taste delicious hot dogs
I smell strawberry ice cream
I feel crunchy leaves.

Stacey Paradise Mafuta (5)
Downs Barn School, Milton Keynes

Autumn Days

I hear whizzing fireworks
I see birds migrating
I taste hot chocolate
I smell smoke
I feel a crunchy leaf.

Amelia Bhalla Rzeznicka (5)
Downs Barn School, Milton Keynes

What senses did you enjoy reading about on these pages? Colour the symbols.

Autumn Colours

I taste jacket potatoes
I smell soup with pumpkins
I hear crackling fireworks
I see birds migrating
I feel crispy leaves falling.

Lexie Woods (5)
Downs Barn School, Milton Keynes

Autumn Days

See the sparkly fireworks
Smell the sticky marshmallows
Taste the creamy hot chocolate
Hear the funfair music
Feel the crunchy leaves.

Kelvin Kuagbenu Adjavon, Yasmeen Samake, Julia, Samuel & Devon (5)
Downs Barn School, Milton Keynes

What senses did you enjoy reading about on these pages? Colour the symbols.

Autumn Is Here

Autumn is here
Crunching leaves and damp air
Blackberries are juicy and very sweet
Apples and red leaves, yellow leaves and orange leaves
And some leaves are brown
Autumn is here.

Ethan Livesey (5)
Holmer Green First School, Buckinghamshire

Autumn Is Here

Autumn is here
I can see the red leaves
The juicy blackberries taste sweet
And juicy apples taste delicious
I feel cold
I hear fireworks at night
Autumn is here.

Charlotte Clark (5)
Holmer Green First School, Buckinghamshire

What senses did you enjoy reading about on these pages? Colour the symbols.

Autumn Is Here

Autumn is here
Leaves fall off the trees
I can feel crunching under my feet
I see pumpkins, orange
I can taste damp air
Autumn is here.

Jack Spiller (5)
Holmer Green First School, Buckinghamshire

Autumn Is Here

Autumn is here
I can hear leaves crunching when I step on them
I can see leaves falling off the trees
Autumn is here.

Isabelle Charlotte Bowring (5)
Holmer Green First School, Buckinghamshire

What senses did you enjoy reading about on these pages? Colour the symbols.

Autumn Is Here

Autumn is here
Green leaves
The crunchy leaves
Yellow, bright leaves
Crispy leaves
Orange, brown leaves
Autumn is here.

Gabriel Shoyombo (5)
Holmer Green First School, Buckinghamshire

Autumn Is Here

Autumn is here
I can hear the damp, crunchy leaves
Yellow leaves
Red leaves
Brown leaves crunchy
Autumn is here.

Loui Hayes (5)
Holmer Green First School, Buckinghamshire

What senses did you enjoy reading about on these pages? Colour the symbols.

Autumn Is Here

Autumn is here
I see leaves falling off the tree
I hear crackling leaves
I smell damp air
Autumn is here.

Ruben Myburgh (5)
Holmer Green First School, Buckinghamshire

Autumn Is Here

Autumn is here
You can see pumpkins down on the ground
I can feel damp air
I can taste the blackberries
I can hear the crunchy leaves
Autumn is here.

Angelica Harker (6)
Holmer Green First School, Buckinghamshire

What senses did you enjoy reading about on these pages? Colour the symbols.

Autumn

Breaking leaves, breaking leaves
Why do they break?
I like leaves
I like autumn
Because it is blowing
Colourful and crackling
I like leaves
I see falling leaves
But why do they turn dry?
I like leaves.

Joshua LeVan (6)
Holmer Green First School, Buckinghamshire

Autumn Leaves

I hear rustling leaves in the trees
I feel hard leaves in my hand
I see red, orange and brown leaves.

Luke Salt (6)
Holmer Green First School, Buckinghamshire

What senses did you enjoy reading about on these pages? Colour the symbols.

Untitled

Autumn leaves crunch and are very dry
I also think they make a crumbly sound
And are hard and bumpy
I hear the leaves falling, wet, swaying
Rustling, crunching, hard, blowing and crackling.

Jessica Lewington (6)
Holmer Green First School, Buckinghamshire

Autumn Colours

Leaves
Autumn
Dry
Rusty
Red
Yellow.

Alex Brown (6)
Holmer Green First School, Buckinghamshire

What senses did you enjoy reading about on these pages? Colour the symbols.

Untitled

I hear rustling, hard and beautiful leaves
I feel crunchy, dry autumn leaves
Smooth, wet and crunching
I see dry, crumbly, crunchy, sweaty
Rusty red, orange and blue leaves.

Meila Farrelly (6)
Holmer Green First School, Buckinghamshire

Untitled

Crunch, crunch, autumn leaves
All rough and good
Some yellow, some red
Crunch, crunch, autumn leaves
Yellow and red
Crunch, crunch, leaves
Bumpy, crunchy, red
And brown, yellow and colourful.

Harry Daly (7)
Holmer Green First School, Buckinghamshire

What senses did you enjoy reading about on these pages? Colour the symbols.

Autumn Leaves

I can feel hard, dry, bumpy, tickly,
Wet, spiky, rough leaves
I can see the falling, yellow, dry, red,
Hard and colourful lovely brown leaves
I can hear crackling, beautiful, crunchy,
Spiky, rustling, tickly leaves.

Eleanor Cowling (6)
Holmer Green First School, Buckinghamshire

Crunchy Leaves

Autumn leaves smell disgusting and crunchy
And look brown and orange
They swish in the wind and crunch
When it rains the leaves
Swish beautifully
The winds blow swiftly.

Eden Souter (6)
Holmer Green First School, Buckinghamshire

What senses did you enjoy reading about on these pages? Colour the symbols.

Untitled

In autumn I can feel
Dry, bumpy, hard and rough leaves
Leaves are very colourful
In autumn I can hear
Swaying, crunching, dry
Red, beautiful, crackling and rustling leaves
In autumn I can see
Yellow, brown, red and orange
It is very beautiful.

Gracie Taylor (6)
Holmer Green First School, Buckinghamshire

Untitled

In autumn I can see swaying leaves
I can hear orange, colourful, rustling
Brown, yellow and crunchy leaves
I can feel dry and crunchy leaves.

Lucy Harris (6)
Holmer Green First School, Buckinghamshire

What senses did you enjoy reading about on these pages? Colour the symbols.

Autumn Is Coming

Crunchy, dry leaves
That's what I can feel in autumn
They look damp, orange, blowing,
Crackling, rough and beautiful
Because they are
Curling, crackling, crunchy and rustling
As I walk around the playground.

Jessica Carr (7)
Holmer Green First School, Buckinghamshire

Untitled

In the autumn the leaves are spiky, rough, tickly and wet
I can see the dry, orange leaves
Red, colourful, swaying and falling
I can hear the leaves
Rustling, crunching and cracking.

Megan Waker (6)
Holmer Green First School, Buckinghamshire

What senses did you enjoy reading about on these pages? Colour the symbols.

My Autumn Shape Poem

I can hear crunchy leaves
I can see leaves swish
I can feel leaves crumble.

Olivia Dunn (6)
Holmer Green First School, Buckinghamshire

My Autumn Shape Poem

I see brown leaves
I hear leaves waving
I feel crunchy leaves
I feel spiky leaves waving
Feeling dry.

Avari Makayla Phipps (6)
Holmer Green First School, Buckinghamshire

My Autumn Poem

I hear a crunching crunch of leaves falling from the trees,
I see red, yellow, brown and orange leaves scattered on the ground,
I feel rustly, hard leaves on the floor around the trees.

Charlie Danielle Allison (6)
Holmer Green First School, Buckinghamshire

What senses did you enjoy reading about on these pages? Colour the symbols.

Autumn

A utumn means Halloween coming soon
U mbrellas get wet while we are dry
T anks and lorries slip on the road while we are on the pavement
U nbuilt buildings get built
M ad stuff starts happening
N uts fall off the tree for the squirrels.

Luke Price (6)
Holmer Green First School, Buckinghamshire

Autumn

A utumn is coming around England
U nder the smooth, soft soil it is crunchy
T he benches are crusty, damp and wet
U mbrellas are here to keep us dry from the rain
M ittens are keeping our cold hands warm on scooters
N ow everyone is getting cold, now we need our coats.

Sienna Faye Wood (6)
Holmer Green First School, Buckinghamshire

What senses did you enjoy reading about on these pages? Colour the symbols.

Autumn

A utumn is coming and the leaves are falling off the trees
U mbrellas are useful because they keep us dry
T rees in autumn - the leaves change colour
U nder the soil is ants
M ice live in the attic
N ice bunny rabbits.

Sophie Morris (6)
Holmer Green First School, Buckinghamshire

Autumn

A utumn is cold
U nder the cold, damp soil there are nocturnal animals
T he combine harvester cuts the grass in autumn
U sing trees is really good because it gives us oxygen
M y tree is bald so you cannot see the beautiful autumn leaves
N obody doesn't like the crunchy leaves.

Abigail Randall (6)
Holmer Green First School, Buckinghamshire

What senses did you enjoy reading about on these pages? Colour the symbols.

Autumn

A is for apples that we eat at harvest
U nder the trees is black, messy soil
T he animals are hibernating ready for winter
U mbrellas keep us dry from the rain
M is for lovely, beautiful Mum
N is for November this year.

Millie Anita Eva Tanner (6)
Holmer Green First School, Buckinghamshire

Autumn

A utumn leaves falling from the tall trees
U nbearable swishy, strong wind
T he animals are all hibernating all through it
U mbrellas keeping you dry from the heavy rain
M ums making the fire warmer so you don't get cold
N uts falling from the trees because the trees are icy cold.

Teo Poulter (6)
Holmer Green First School, Buckinghamshire

What senses did you enjoy reading about on these pages? Colour the symbols.

Autumn

A t autumn all the leaves fall
U nderground animals hibernate
T he rain is tumbling down
U p in the trees live squirrels
M umbling squirrels in the trees
N anny says I can have a present in autumn.

Alexander Taylor (6)
Holmer Green First School, Buckinghamshire

Autumn

A utumn crunchy leaves
U nderground creatures hibernate
T he howling wind blows
U nderground creatures sleep
M isty wind is blowing around
N oisy birds are whistling.

Mediha Dawood (6)
Holmer Green First School, Buckinghamshire

What senses did you enjoy reading about on these pages? Colour the symbols.

Autumn

A utumn crunchy, crumbly leaves fall off the trees
U mbrellas keep the wet, soggy rain away
T he green trees don't have many crunchy leaves
U nder the cover we keep warm, cosy and dry
M y bed is warm and snuggly away from the cold
N oisy, colourful, spiky leaves fall off the trees.

Holly Jessop (6)
Holmer Green First School, Buckinghamshire

Autumn

A utumn leaves falling from the wavy trees
U nder the trees are crispy leaves
T he leaves are falling and are crunchy and crispy
U mbrellas keep us dry when it is raining
M ud is wet
N is for November all near and rare.

Lexie Johnson (6)
Holmer Green First School, Buckinghamshire

What senses did you enjoy reading about on these pages? Colour the symbols.

Autumn Is Here

Autumn is here
Leaves are falling to the ground
Smoking bonfires
Leaves are sticky
Red juicy apples
Fireworks go *boom, boom!*
Autumn is here.

Marley Smith (5)
Holmer Green First School, Buckinghamshire

Autumn Is Here

Autumn is here
Golden leaves
Pumpkin pie
Wind blowing
Hot dog and ketchup
Spiky shell
Autumn is here.

Daisy Sharp (5)
Holmer Green First School, Buckinghamshire

What senses did you enjoy reading about on these pages? Colour the symbols.

Autumn Is Here

Autumn is here
Red and yellow leaves
Leaves rustling
Smoky bonfire
Juicy apples
Spiky conker shells
Autumn is here.

Alex Smith (5)
Holmer Green First School, Buckinghamshire

Autumn Is Here

Autumn is here
Leaves falling
Smoky fire
Wind
Crunchy carrots
Spiky conker shell
Autumn is here.

Lewis Vincent Norris (5)
Holmer Green First School, Buckinghamshire

What senses did you enjoy reading about on these pages? Colour the symbols.

Autumn Is Here

Autumn is here
Swirling leaves
Smoky bonfire
Rustling leaves
Crunchy apples
Smooth conkers
Autumn is here.

Jessica Harper (5)
Holmer Green First School, Buckinghamshire

Autumn Is Here

Autumn is here
Golden leaves
Smoky bonfire
Crunchy leaves
Chilly wind
Soft conkers
Autumn is here.

Toby Heath (5)
Holmer Green First School, Buckinghamshire

What senses did you enjoy reading about on these pages? Colour the symbols.

Autumn Is Here

Autumn is here
Brown conker
Crunchy leaves
Smoky fire
Yummy hot dog
Prickly shell
Autumn is here.

Jack Hubbard (5)
Holmer Green First School, Buckinghamshire

Autumn Is Here

Autumn is here
Changing colours
Pumpkins soup
Crunchy leaves
Chewy toffee apples
Wind blowing in my face
Autumn is here.

Orlaigh Farrow (5)
Holmer Green First School, Buckinghamshire

What senses did you enjoy reading about on these pages? Colour the symbols.

Autumn Is Here

Autumn is here
Crunchy golden leaves
Rustling brown leaves
Conkers falling off the trees
Sweet flowers
Smoking bonfires
Autumn is here.

Caitlyn Rose Davidson (6)
Holmer Green First School, Buckinghamshire

Autumn Is Here

Autumn is here
Leaves are tumbling down
Smelly bonfire
I hear banging fireworks
I taste sausage hot dogs
I touch crunchy leaves
Autumn is here.

Lily Dell (5)
Holmer Green First School, Buckinghamshire

What senses did you enjoy reading about on these pages? Colour the symbols.

Autumn Is Here

Autumn is here
Leaves floating down
Smoky bonfire
Crunchy leaves
Tasty hot dogs
Spiky conker shells
Autumn is here.

Harry James Anson (6)
Holmer Green First School, Buckinghamshire

Autumn Is Here

Autumn is here
Leaves falling from the trees
Smells from the farm
Falling leaves spinning on the ground
The cold wind
Spiky conker shell
Autumn is here.

Joshua William Clark (6)
Holmer Green First School, Buckinghamshire

What senses did you enjoy reading about on these pages? Colour the symbols.

Firework Poem

I'm a little rocket,
Whooshing through the sky,
Precious as a locket,
Whirling, shooting and darting as I fly.

Children eating yummy hot dogs,
Swirling their sparklers in the air,
Whistle, bang, pop go the bonfire logs,
I'm shimmery and beautiful like lights at a fair.

Reggie Lloyd (6)
Holy Trinity CE (VA) Primary School, Taunton

Firework Poem

Fireworks bang,
Sparklers sparkle,
Bonfire crackle,
Sausages sizzle,
Sweet chocolate,
Fireworks twinkle,
Twinkle like a star.

Robyn Ash-Smith (6)
Holy Trinity CE (VA) Primary School, Taunton

What senses did you enjoy reading about on these pages? Colour the symbols.

Firework Poem

Yellow sparking fireworks,
Booming in the sky,
Rainbow colours glow in the cold dark night,
Yellow, purple, blue
Boom, bang, pop.

Smoke is blowing in my eyes,
They give me tears,
Hot dogs on my red BBQ.

Halle Taylor (6)
Holy Trinity CE (VA) Primary School, Taunton

Firework Poem

Fire, fire fireworks,
I love fireworks in the sky,
Beautiful colours up high,
Eating fizzy sweets inside.

Smelly fireworks wafting up my nose,
The crackling sound of the bonfire in my ears.

Lottie Elizabeth Brunt (6)
Holy Trinity CE (VA) Primary School, Taunton

What senses did you enjoy reading about on these pages? Colour the symbols.

Firework Poem

Swirl, twirl goes the rocket,
Fizzy Coke wafts up my nose,
Loud like a bomb went a firecracker,
Warm gloves and hats,
Colourful lights fly in the night-time sky,
I stare and sigh,
'I wish the moon would come out tonight.'

Fiona Dumlao (6)
Holy Trinity CE (VA) Primary School, Taunton

Firework Poem

Red rocket racing by
Zooming around in the air
Lovely taste of hot dogs in my mouth
Fireworks shooting north and south.

Tom Hebditch (6)
Holy Trinity CE (VA) Primary School, Taunton

What senses did you enjoy reading about on these pages? Colour the symbols.

Firework Poem

Rocket pocket,
Fizz, whizz,
Popping candy,
Yummy popcorn in my tummy,
Bash, crash,
Night lights,
Yawn, yawn,
Time for bed.

Christopher Cowdell (6)
Holy Trinity CE (VA) Primary School, Taunton

Firework Poem

Fireworks make lots of sound,
Like *pop, bang, boom,*
Rainbow colours glow in the dark.

I hear screaming in my head and ears,
Smoky smell on my T-shirt and near my eyes.

Aleks Zuchowicz (7)
Holy Trinity CE (VA) Primary School, Taunton

What senses did you enjoy reading about on these pages? Colour the symbols.

Firework Poem

Boom, crash go the fireworks,
Banging in my ears,
Blue, gold, purple and silver
Colours I see here.

Silver sparkles smelling hot,
Tasty hot dogs too
Salty popcorn and popping candy
Chocolate drinks for you.

Chloe Purcell (6)
Holy Trinity CE (VA) Primary School, Taunton

Firework Poem

The taste of sizzling smoky sausages on the BBQ,
Smells like popping candy,
They're very noisy in my ears,
Bang, bash, crash, smash.

Jayden Jack Shortland (7)
Holy Trinity CE (VA) Primary School, Taunton

What senses did you enjoy reading about on these pages? Colour the symbols.

The Autumn Wood Poem

Autumn days can be spooky and cruel
The spiders are as black as prancing crows
Mossy trees hard as stone
Trees waving in the freezing breeze
The sunlight reflecting on the floor and trees
The smell of fresh water from the river and leaves.

Chloe Jaye Shopland (7)
Knights Templar First School, Watchet

My Magnificent Poem

I taste hot chocolate
I hear the river flowing
I feel the rough bark on the tall trees
I see the spiky leaves on the bushes
I smell the smell of stew
I taste the taste of squishy marshmallows
I hear the red and yellow leaves crunching under my feet
I can touch the cold water in the river.

Lloyd Harding (7)
Knights Templar First School, Watchet

What senses did you enjoy reading about on these pages? Colour the symbols.

Autumn Poem

A utumn is the best day ever!
U se some crunching leaves to make a picture
T oday I will play with the yellow, orange and red trees
U mbrellas can protect you from the spiky leaves that have fallen from the trees
M ysterious leaves can be found in autumn
N uts fall off the trees when it is autumn.

Sizhu Chen (7)
Knights Templar First School, Watchet

Autumn Poem

I can hear the fantastic breeze blowing
I can touch the prickly hard bark
I can see a beautiful woodpecker
I can taste the jolly smell of apple pie
I can feel the sparkly wind flying.

Malachi Smyth (7)
Knights Templar First School, Watchet

What senses did you enjoy reading about on these pages? Colour the symbols.

Autumn Crunch

I can hear the rustling of the leaves
I can hear the trees shaking
I can hear the crunching leaves
I can see the wet leaves on the floor
I can taste the roaring bonfires
I can taste the hot chocolate on a cold day
I can see all the leaves in the dirty puddles
I can see all the leaves falling off the trees
I can see all the rain dropping on the floor like thunder
I can see all the rain going through the roof.

Cruize Edwards (7)
Knights Templar First School, Watchet

In Autumn

In autumn I can see the beautiful, colourful leaves
In autumn I can feel the wet grass
In autumn I can hear the cold wind blowing in my ears
In autumn I can taste water from the rain.

Daniel Evans-White (6)
Knights Templar First School, Watchet

What senses did you enjoy reading about on these pages? Colour the symbols.

Autumn

I feel leaves crunching under my feet
I can smell bonfires wherever I go
Touching trees when I am sad
I see birds when I look out of my window
I taste marshmallows when I'm playing with my friends
I can feel the wind blowing in my face
When I get chilly I think of hot chocolate.

Lewis Clavey (6)
Knights Templar First School, Watchet

In The Woods

I can pet the squirrel in the woods
I can taste the autumn breeze
I can hear the birds in the trees
I can smell the autumn smells
I can see the birds in the trees.

Charlie Mark Penny (7)
Knights Templar First School, Watchet

What senses did you enjoy reading about on these pages? Colour the symbols.

Autumn

I can hear the rustling on the trees
I can taste Yorkshire puddings
I can taste hot chocolate
I can taste apple pie
I can taste a cup of tea
I can smell my roast dinner cooking in the oven
I can see the yellow and orange leaves falling from the trees
I can feel the wind blowing in my face.

Millie Johnson (7)
Knights Templar First School, Watchet

Autumn Sense Poem

I feel the rough and tough bark on the trees
I hear scrunching leaves under my cold feet
I see red, orange and yellow leaves under my freezing feet
I taste hot chocolate and Mum baking chocolate cake
I smell cake in the cold breeze.

Olivia Grace Davis (6)
Knights Templar First School, Watchet

What senses did you enjoy reading about on these pages? Colour the symbols.

Alana's Autumn Poem

A utumn days is when pink leaves fall off tall trees
U sing blankets to keep you warm with hot chocolate
T aste of hot roast dinner with cold ice cream for tea
U sing umbrellas for rainy days so we don't get wet
M ums are saying bye in the freezing cold mornings
N ights are as wet as melted snow.

Alana Bulpin (7)
Knights Templar First School, Watchet

Autumn

I hear the crunchy crisp leaves under my feet
I can touch the rough bumpy bark of the trees
I can see the bare brown trees
I can smell fires
I can taste hot chocolate.

Phoebe Pope (7)
Knights Templar First School, Watchet

What senses did you enjoy reading about on these pages? Colour the symbols.

Finley's Fabulous Poem

I hear the leaves crunching under my feet
I taste yummy hot chocolate in my mouth
I see rubbish flowing on the floor
I hold the yummy hot chocolate in my hand
I smell the damp leaves starting to grow.

Finley Kidner (7)
Knights Templar First School, Watchet

Autumn Poem

A utumn days when the leaves are colourful
U nder my feet are scattered leaves
T aste of hot chocolate when I go home
U mbrellas full of leaves just like a ladybird
M um cooks a lemon and sugar as hot as water
N othing like beautiful hot chocolate.

Oscar Jack Powis (6)
Knights Templar First School, Watchet

What senses did you enjoy reading about on these pages? Colour the symbols.

Cold Days

A scattering of leaves in my face
U mbrellas put up in the hard rain
T oys being played with outside
U s going for walks in the leaves
M um making roast dinner
N ow this is the best day ever.

Ethan Palmer (7)
Knights Templar First School, Watchet

Autumn

I can feel leaves dropping on my head
I can hear the wind blowing
I can feel the wind on my face
I can feel the coldness.

Samuel Isaacs (7)
Knights Templar First School, Watchet

What senses did you enjoy reading about on these pages? Colour the symbols.

Happiness

Happiness smells like sweet summer
Happiness tastes like chewy, crunchy chocolate
Happiness looks like a warm night
Happiness feels like a warm pillow
Happiness sounds like a mum singing
Winter smells like a drop dripping
Winter looks like a feather floating
Winter tastes like a roast dinner
Winter feels like a cube melting
Winter sounds like music
School smells like lovely flowers
School looks like a soft blanket.

Connie Smith (6)
Marsh Gibbon CE School, Bicester

Happiness

Happiness sounds beautiful
It's calm and fast and loud
Happiness smells like summer and lollipops and candyfloss
Happiness feels like cold icicles hanging from above your window
Happiness tastes like roast dinner and Yorkshire pudding.

Tom Hide (7)
Marsh Gibbon CE School, Bicester

What senses did you enjoy reading about on these pages? Colour the symbols.

Autumn

Autumn smells like fireworks
Autumn sounds like conkers banging on the pavement
Autumn looks like orange, red and brown
Autumn tastes like water, it is nice.

Rayaan Miya (5)
Millbrook Combined School, High Wycombe

Autumn

Autumn smells like smoke hanging in the air
Autumn sounds like banging in the sky
Autumn looks like colours blasting in the sky
Autumn tastes like chocolate
Autumn feels soft.

Usman Nawaz (5)
Millbrook Combined School, High Wycombe

Autumn

Autumn smells like ice cream
Autumn sounds like fireworks
Autumn tastes like muffins
Autumn is full of leaves
Autumn looks soft.

Tomasz Tomczyk (5)
Millbrook Combined School, High Wycombe

What senses did you enjoy reading about on these pages? Colour the symbols.

Autumn

Autumn smells like burning fire
Autumn looks like falling leaves
Autumn feels soft
Autumn sounds like conkers falling.

Amelia Mozdzierska (5)
Millbrook Combined School, High Wycombe

Autumn

Autumn smells like bonfire smoke
Autumn sounds like banging sparks
Autumn looks like colourful fireworks.

Sufyan Hussain (5)
Millbrook Combined School, High Wycombe

Autumn

Autumn smells like a bonfire.
Autumn sounds like leaves falling off a tree.
Autumn looks like the leaves that are bright and colourful.

Wiktoria Redzinska (5)
Millbrook Combined School, High Wycombe

What senses did you enjoy reading about on these pages? Colour the symbols.

Fear

Fear is black, white and grey like the war in the olden days
Fear smells like dirty dogs eating big bones from a big dark shop
Fear tastes like disgusting mushrooms, disgusting!
Fear feels like dirty drains with soggy cans in
Fear sounds like robbers being chased by police cars.

Esmee Kennelly (6)
Newton Poppleford Primary School, Sidmouth

Excited

Excited tastes like sweet mango and lemonade sweets
Excited smells like the newly cut grass with rain on it
Excited feels like the lively multicoloured tulips
Excited looks like all the different coloured fireworks on Bonfire Night
Excited sounds like me screaming inside myself.

Martha Cox (6)
Newton Poppleford Primary School, Sidmouth

What senses did you enjoy reading about on these pages? Colour the symbols.

Hopeful

Hopeful is red like the flowers
Hopeful - I can smell like juicy air
Hopeful - soft, amazing sand
Hopeful - I can see the tall trees
Hopeful - a family playing in the sea.

Kyla Leah Hall (6)
Newton Poppleford Primary School, Sidmouth

I Hate Anger

Anger is red like a big burning bonfire
Anger smells like a big smelly bog
Anger tastes like a mouthful of flaming fire
Anger feels like a wet and soggy loaf of bread
Anger looks like a monster lurking outside your window
Anger sounds like a medal clicking as sharp as a spike.

Charlotte Player (7)
Newton Poppleford Primary School, Sidmouth

What senses did you enjoy reading about on these pages? Colour the symbols.

Embarrassment

Embarrassment is light blue like a single tear dropping down
Embarrassment smells like booing at you
Embarrassment tastes like blackberries sliming the juice on you
Embarrassment feels like fire burning through you
Embarrassment looks like a clown crawling on the floor
Embarrassment sounds like a bunny hopping in a fire.

Alice Ridgway (6)
Newton Poppleford Primary School, Sidmouth

Excited

Excited is light blue like the fresh blue sky
Excited smells like the fresh green grass
Excited tastes like sweet-smelling porridge with sugar
Excited feels like lots of nerves in your tummy
Excited looks like a massive crowd cheering at you
Excited sounds like happy crying and sweet laughing.

Isabel Davies (6)
Newton Poppleford Primary School, Sidmouth

What senses did you enjoy reading about on these pages? Colour the symbols.

Amazement

Amazement is blue like the sky.
Amazement smells like new oranges.
Amazement tastes like air at the beach.
Amazement feels cold like the cold sea.
Amazement looks like a 3-year-old's cartwheels.
Amazement sounds like bells at the church.

Emily Robin Tubbs (6)
Newton Poppleford Primary School, Sidmouth

Sadness

Sadness is like the green trees
Sadness smells like disgusting socks
Sadness tastes like disgusting brown mouldy bread with blackberries
Sadness sounds like the wind, wolves howling in the trees
Sadness looks like a dead bird on the dark road.

Coco Bond (6)
Newton Poppleford Primary School, Sidmouth

What senses did you enjoy reading about on these pages? Colour the symbols.

Happy

Happy is light blue like the sky
Happy smells like Haribos
Happy tastes so nice like lavender
Happy feels so happy like the teachers
Happy looks like bells dinging in the church
Happy sounds like the sea splashing.

Olivia Stanley (6)
Newton Poppleford Primary School, Sidmouth

Disgust

Disgust is green like the grass
Disgust smells like smelly socks
Disgust tastes like burnt food
Disgust feels like a worm on my head
Disgust looks like a dead bird's blood
Disgust sounds like an aeroplane taking off.

Imogen Norman (6)
Newton Poppleford Primary School, Sidmouth

What senses did you enjoy reading about on these pages? Colour the symbols.

Excited

Excited is glittery sparkle on a party dress
Excited smells like amazing sweets
Excited tastes like fresh milkshake
Excited feels like super soft things
Excited looks like melted chocolate
Excited sounds like special bells.

Jessie Stone (6)
Newton Poppleford Primary School, Sidmouth

Angry

Anger is red like apples
Anger smells like fire
Anger tastes like mushrooms
Anger feels like a war
Anger looks like red blood dripping down my arm
Anger sounds like Thomas shouting at my mum.

Jonno Fletcher (6)
Newton Poppleford Primary School, Sidmouth

What senses did you enjoy reading about on these pages? Colour the symbols.

Untitled

An iguana smells like a lemon
An iguana looks like a pear but it isn't
An iguana feels as hard as a pebble
An iguana sounds crunchy like walking on snow
An iguana tastes as hard as toast.

Evan Beavis (5)
Newton Poppleford Primary School, Sidmouth

A Strawberry

Strawberries sound silent
Strawberries feel squishy like my teddy bear
Strawberries look pale like my dog
Strawberries smell like my flowers
Strawberries taste juicy like my little pear.

Martha Cox (5)
Newton Poppleford Primary School, Sidmouth

What senses did you enjoy reading about on these pages? Colour the symbols.

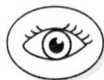

Blackberry

A blackberry feels very bumpy
A blackberry looks black and thorny when it's on a bush
A blackberry smells very sweet
A blackberry tastes sour
A blackberry sounds soft and has a faint crunch in my mouth.

Oskabah Leeson-Kings (6)
Newton Poppleford Primary School, Sidmouth

Food

I like hearing sizzling sausages,
I like touching soft cheese,
I like seeing colourful jelly,
I like smelling delicious orange juice,
I like tasting spicy sausages.

Kaori Daniels (5)
North Hinksey CE Primary School, Oxford

What senses did you enjoy reading about on these pages? Colour the symbols.

Popcorn

Popcorn smells sweet
It sounds like fireworks
It feels bumpy
It tastes crunchy
It looks bubbly.

River Louise Collier (6)
Offa's Mead Academy, Chepstow

Popcorn

Popcorn smells sweet
Popcorn sounds like fireworks
Popcorn feels like soft balls
Popcorn feels like a piece of chicken in a ball!
Popcorn tastes like butter.

Sophie Christina Millicent Rees (6)
Offa's Mead Academy, Chepstow

What senses did you enjoy reading about on these pages? Colour the symbols.

Popcorn

Popcorn smells like smoke
Popcorn looks like little stones
Popcorn feels soft
Popcorn sounds like *pop, pop, pop*
Popcorn smells like toast
I love popcorn!

Hannah Woodall (5)
Offa's Mead Academy, Chepstow

Popcorn

I can smell sweets
I can hear bangs
I can see golden teeth
I can feel bumps
I can taste sweets
Yum-yum!

Charlie Hale (5)
Offa's Mead Academy, Chepstow

What senses did you enjoy reading about on these pages? Colour the symbols.

Popcorn

Popcorn smells yummy
Popcorn feels hard
Popcorn smells very good
Because it tastes crunchy
I like popcorn yum-yum!

Chenel Slater (5)
Offa's Mead Academy, Chepstow

A Winter Day

I can see children playing in the cold, icy snow
I can hear crunchy, crackly footsteps
I can feel the freezing cold snowflakes when they fall on my tongue
I can smell the fresh air.

Imogen Mary Cima (5)
Peppard CE Primary School, Henley-on-Thames

What senses did you enjoy reading about on these pages? Colour the symbols.

Windy Senses

I can hear the wind howling
Hissing, wishing silently, wailing, whining wind
I can feel the breezy, blowing windy wind
I can see the whirling, hooping
Twirling tornado wind
I can smell the wind
The watery windy air blowing
I can taste the wind's breezy breath
I can feel the wind's lips making my face cold.

Dylan Blake Mole (6)
Peppard CE Primary School, Henley-on-Thames

Shiny Snow

I can see the white silky snow quietly falling into my shoe
I can hear the crunching snow heavily coming down on my nose
I can smell the heavy hot chocolate waiting for me
I can taste the crunchy snow dropping on my tongue.

Sienna Keyte (6)
Peppard CE Primary School, Henley-on-Thames

What senses did you enjoy reading about on these pages? Colour the symbols.

Christmas And Snow

I can see silky, swirling snowflakes playing elegantly and quietly
I can hear Father Christmas say, 'Ho, ho, ho!'
And jingle bells jingling and Christmas carols too
I can feel silky, slippery ice
I can taste warm, steaming hot chocolate
As brown as tree bark
And every sip is a magical Christmas dream
I can smell crispy, crunchy roast dinner.

Isobel Sue Swanwick (6)
Peppard CE Primary School, Henley-on-Thames

Bright Sun

I can see the bright sun
I can hear the birds cheeping
I can feel the hot blinding sun
I can taste the sweet ice cream
I can smell the sweet wind blowing.

Ruby Turner (5)
Peppard CE Primary School, Henley-on-Thames

What senses did you enjoy reading about on these pages? Colour the symbols.

My Senses In The Snow

I can see the icy-cold snow crunching beneath my feet
I can hear people throwing snowballs at people
I can smell the cold air and the snow
I can see snow shivering in my hands
I can taste the snow shivering in my mouth
I can feel the cold snow between my fingers.

Josie Tolhurst-Wilson (5)
Peppard CE Primary School, Henley-on-Thames

The Snow Storm

I can see the crispy snow
I can hear the footsteps in the snow
I can feel the crunching snow
I can taste the silky snow
I can smell the icy snow.

Harrison Webb (5)
Peppard CE Primary School, Henley-on-Thames

What senses did you enjoy reading about on these pages? Colour the symbols.

The Weather

I can see the silky snow
I can hear the crunchy snow
I can feel the cold snow
I can taste the snowflakes
I can smell the lovely, creamy snow that's really cold.

Jake Wilde (6)
Peppard CE Primary School, Henley-on-Thames

A Snowy Christmas

I can see some children playing in the soft, silky snow
I can hear the children stopping in the dripping snow
I can taste the snow falling on my tongue
I can feel the crunchy smooth snow
I can smell the frosty, silent snow.

Astrid Waite (6)
Peppard CE Primary School, Henley-on-Thames

What senses did you enjoy reading about on these pages? Colour the symbols.

The Snowy Weather

I can see my hot chocolate in my big house
I can hear children playing in the white snow
I can feel the crunchy snow
I can taste the cold snow
I can smell white snow.

Max Claridge (5)
Peppard CE Primary School, Henley-on-Thames

The Sunny Day

I can see the train in the hot sun
I can feel hot metal
I can taste hot water
I can hear the birds sing
I can see flowers on the green grass.

Joseph Prince (6)
Peppard CE Primary School, Henley-on-Thames

What senses did you enjoy reading about on these pages? Colour the symbols.

The Icy Snow

I can see the swirling, cold, white, silent, silky snow
I can hear the quiet, breezy, twirling, whooshing cold snow
I can smell the yummy mince pies
I can feel the dropping, swaying, silent, soft snowflakes falling on my tongue.

Daisy Millard (7)
Peppard CE Primary School, Henley-on-Thames

White Snow

I can see the soft, silky, fluffy, crumbly snow
I can hear the shimmering, glittery birds tweeting in the trees
I can smell scrummy, yummy Christmas dinner
I can taste the cold, wet snow
I can feel cold, wet, fluffy snow.

Olivia Garland (6)
Peppard CE Primary School, Henley-on-Thames

What senses did you enjoy reading about on these pages? Colour the symbols.

The Snow

I can feel the crunchy, cold, silky snow
I can hear my next-door neighbours crunching and munching their
Christmas dinner
I can smell the smoke of fire
I can taste the Christmas dinner that I am munching up
I can see the kids opening their presents.

Freddie Jelowitz (6)
Peppard CE Primary School, Henley-on-Thames

My Garden

I can see a beautiful, shiny, sparkly, dark green palm tree
I can taste a juicy, sweet, apple-flavoured icy lolly
I can touch a spiky, prickly, red rose's thorns
I can hear a tweet from a lovely lime-green woodpecker
I can smell a beautiful planted lonely flower.

Alfie Pease (7)
St Blasius CE Primary Academy, Shanklin

What senses did you enjoy reading about on these pages? Colour the symbols.

My Garden

I can hear a small, buzzing bee
I can touch nice, green, fresh, short grass
I can see a green bush
I can smell a nice, strong lolly
I can taste a mint chocolate ice cream.

Lily Smith (7)
St Blasius CE Primary Academy, Shanklin

My Garden

I can see a tall, brown, green, leafy, thick tree
I can taste lots of black, squashy, juicy, yummy, bumpy blackberries
I can touch green, long, fresh, crunchy, munchy grassy grass
I can smell red and yellow petals and long, pretty flowers
I can hear tiny, spotty, round, small, crawling bugs.

Eloise Barnes (7)
St Blasius CE Primary Academy, Shanklin

What senses did you enjoy reading about on these pages? Colour the symbols.

My Garden

I can see a buzzing, yellow and black stinging bee
I can taste a ham sandwich
I can smell pink and purple flowers
I can touch a bouncing blue and green ball and a spiky brown tree
I can hear a chirping bird and buzzing yellow and black stinging bees.

Max Wenman (6)
St Blasius CE Primary Academy, Shanklin

My Garden

I can hear a seagull squawking
I can touch fresh, long, green grass
I can see a brown and green baby tree
I can smell some big, dark green leaves on a big, tall tree
I can taste a tasty, sweet, long, strawberry lolly.

Megan Rose Copsey (7)
St Blasius CE Primary Academy, Shanklin

What senses did you enjoy reading about on these pages? Colour the symbols.

My Garden

I smell flowers
I smell fresh, green grass
I taste crunchy crisps
I taste a blackberry too
I see fluttering birds
I see a running dog
I hear soft music
I hear snoozing Grandad
I touch beautiful daisies
I touch soft, green grass.

Angel Louise Perkins (6)
St Blasius CE Primary Academy, Shanklin

My Garden

I can see the beautiful blue sky
I can smell the lovely red, prickly roses
I can hear the buzzing of a black and yellow bee softly in my ear
I can taste barbecued sizzling sausage
I can touch my net of my trampoline.

Finlay Diffey
St Blasius CE Primary Academy, Shanklin

What senses did you enjoy reading about on these pages? Colour the symbols.

My Garden

I can taste medium chocolate, thin, crumbly, crunchy biscuits
I can see a big, red and black, bouncy trampoline
I can touch the short, green, sharp grass
I can hear a loud, fast, little lawn mower
I can smell pretty, small, orange and green flowers sitting in their beds.

Charlie Gomm (7)
St Blasius CE Primary Academy, Shanklin

My Garden

I smell ice cream, it is so good I should have to eat it all
I can hear a baby crying and crying
I can smell a cake, all chocolatey sweet
I can touch rock with my foot, all hard and rough.

Poppy Wittman (6)
St Blasius CE Primary Academy, Shanklin

What senses did you enjoy reading about on these pages? Colour the symbols.

My Garden

I can smell flowers
I can see a big pot
I can taste a cake
I can hear birds tweeting
I can feel a dog
I can taste a doughnut
I can feel a cat
I can smell a cat
I can hear music
I can see a bird
I can see a cat
I can see a dog.

Gracie-Mai Chambers (6)
St Blasius CE Primary Academy, Shanklin

Untitled

I can see a donkey
I can taste a bit of cake
I can touch some paint
I can hear a cricket
I can smell perfume.

Oscar Dugard-Craig (6)
St Blasius CE Primary Academy, Shanklin

What senses did you enjoy reading about on these pages? Colour the symbols.

My Garden

I can smell barbecues and flowers
I can taste sausages
I can hear grass being cut
I can touch a hard, colourful table
I can see tall trees
I can hear laughing children
I can feel summertime.

Riley King (6)
St Blasius CE Primary Academy, Shanklin

My Garden

I can smell flowers
I can smell barbecues
I can see a beautiful, lovely flower
I can hear a cricket
I can touch a bouncy metal trampoline.

Leigh Honey (6)
St Blasius CE Primary Academy, Shanklin

What senses did you enjoy reading about on these pages? Colour the symbols.

My Garden

I can see bugs on the grass
I can taste jam sandwiches
I can smell chocolate cake
I can touch a soft kitten
I can hear a spoon stirring ice tea.

Ethan-James Mennell (6)
St Blasius CE Primary Academy, Shanklin

Untitled

I can hear a car
I can touch a tree
I can taste some barbecue food
I can smell barbecue food
I can see grass being cut.

Tyler Webb (7)
St Blasius CE Primary Academy, Shanklin

What senses did you enjoy reading about on these pages? Colour the symbols.

Through The Door

Open the door, what can you see?
Fluffy black cat,
Flapping, pretty flowers.

Open the door, what can you hear?
Dripping, wet rain,
Pretty, tweeting birds.

Open the door, what can you smell?
Fresh, big air,
Wet, long grass.

Agnes Purling (5)
Shute Community Primary School, Axminster

Through The Shiny Brown Door

Open the shiny, brown door, what can you see?
Beautiful, sparkly flowers,
Shiny, green grass,
Shimmering, yellow sunflowers.

Open the shiny, brown door, what can you hear?
Wavy, beautiful trees,
Loud, noisy children,
Zooming, fast cars.

Open the shiny, brown door, what can you smell?
Fresh, good grass,
Noisy, loud children,
Delicious, yummy barbecue.

Freya Clark (6)
Shute Community Primary School, Axminster

What senses did you enjoy reading about on these pages? Colour the symbols.

The Beach

Open the hut door, what can you see?
Lovely, golden sand,
Crystal-blue sea.

Open the hut door, what can you hear?
Cheerful, nice children,
Crashing, noisy waves.

Open the hut door, what can you smell?
Salty, sweet fish and chips,
Fresh, wonderful seawater.

Oliver Love (6)
Shute Community Primary School, Axminster

The Fun Beach

Open the arcade door, what can you see?
Sparkling, blue sea,
Shiny, gold sand.

Open the arcade door, what can you hear?
Squawking, screeching seagulls,
Noisy, loud arcade.

Open the arcade door, what can you smell?
Delicious fish and chips,
Salty, blue seawater.

Lily R (5)
Shute Community Primary School, Axminster

What senses did you enjoy reading about on these pages? Colour the symbols.

In The Wood

Open the tent door, what can you see?
Soft, strong deer,
Tall, brown trees.

Open the tent door, what can you hear?
Loud, fluffy squirrel,
Loud, fluffy birds.

Open the tent door, what can you smell?
Smoky bonfire,
Sloppy, brown mud.

Pippa Clarkson (7)
Shute Community Primary School, Axminster

The Secret Wood

Open the window, what can you see?
Barky, brown trees,
Rotten, poisonous mushrooms,
Sloppy, sticky mud.

Open the window, what can you hear?
Crunching, green leaves,
Swishing, noisy trees,
Stomping, thumping feet.

Open the window, what can you smell?
Furry, stinky foxes,
Stomping, big deer.

Grace Clarkson (7)
Shute Community Primary School, Axminster

What senses did you enjoy reading about on these pages? Colour the symbols.

In My Garden

Open the window, what can you see?
Big, bouncy trampoline,
Old, resting tree house beam.

Open the window, what can you hear?
Rustling, swaying trees,
Tweeting, twooting birds.

Open the window, what can you smell?
Fresh, cold air,
Green, clean grass.

Tia Bowman (6)
Shute Community Primary School, Axminster

The Scary Wood Poem

Open the tree house door, what can you see?
Long, rough, white branches,
Crystal-blue sky.

Open the tree house door, what can you hear?
Swishing, green leaves on trees,
Tweeting, big birds.

Open the tree house door, what can you smell?
Wet, black mud,
Sweet, glossy tree sap.

April Nex (6)
Shute Community Primary School, Axminster

What senses did you enjoy reading about on these pages? Colour the symbols.

Through The House Window

Open the tree house, what can you see?
Red, tall mushrooms,
Lively, scruffy dogs.

Open the tree house, what can you hear?
Falling, crunchy leaves,
Tweeting, noisy birds.

Open the tree house, what can you smell?
Horrible, stinky bonfire,
Sweet, lovely sap.

Greg L (6)
Shute Community Primary School, Axminster

Through The Window

Open the window, what can you see?
Pink, beautiful flowers,
White, black smudge.

Open the window, what can you hear?
Beautiful tweeting birds,
Swishing, swaying trees.

Open the window, what can you smell?
Nice, fresh air,
Nice, yummy barbecue.

Lyra Jenkin (5)
Shute Community Primary School, Axminster

What senses did you enjoy reading about on these pages? Colour the symbols.

The Football Stadium

The football stadium sounds like a crowd roaring
The football stadium tastes like Coke and chocolate marshmallows
The football stadium smells like men's perfume
The football stadium feels like a cold ball
The football stadium looks like goals.

Aveer Obhrai (7)
Thorpe House Pre-Prep School, Gerrards Cross

Watermelon

Watermelon looks like a football
Watermelon smells like fresh flowers
Watermelon feels like it is cold
Watermelon tastes like it is good.

Miles Gauguier (6)
Thorpe House Pre-Prep School, Gerrards Cross

The House

My house sounds like my dad's car coming into the drive
My house smells nice like a swimming pool
My house feels like me cuddling my teddy bear
My house tastes like jelly
My house looks like a square of chocolate and everything else is sweet.

Ollie Levy (7)
Thorpe House Pre-Prep School, Gerrards Cross

What senses did you enjoy reading about on these pages? Colour the symbols.

The Sea

It looks like colourful fish and creepy sharks
It smells fresh and fishy
It feels like a watery pond
It sounds like waves that go smash on the cliffs
It tastes like fish and blood because the shark ate them.

Yuvraaj Sandhu (6)
Thorpe House Pre-Prep School, Gerrards Cross

Toy Shop

The toy shop looks like a squidgy fat pig
The toy shop feels like marshmallows
The toy shop sounds like a buzzing bee
The toy shop tastes like a big bat.

Harry Chapoulet (7)
Thorpe House Pre-Prep School, Gerrards Cross

What senses did you enjoy reading about on these pages? Colour the symbols.

A Swimming Poem

Swimming sounds like crowds cheering
Swimming looks like annoying people
Swimming smells like chlorine
Swimming feels like a soft bed
Swimming tastes like watermelon.

Jayden James Butcher (7)
Thorpe House Pre-Prep School, Gerrards Cross

A Kitten Poem

Kittens look like cute, cuddly cubs
Kittens feel like fluffy, cuddly carpets
Kittens sound like loud miaowing baby lions
Kittens taste like salty, slippery fish
Kittens smell like yummy fish fingers.

Archie James Shawcross (7)
Thorpe House Pre-Prep School, Gerrards Cross

What senses did you enjoy reading about on these pages? Colour the symbols.

A Christmas Poem

Christmas sounds like Santa saying, 'Ho, Ho, Ho! Merry Christmas!' and sleigh bells with excited children,
Christmas feels like people opening exciting presents,
Christmas tastes like turkey and mince pies,
Christmas looks like shiny and beautiful Christmas trees with twinkling baubles and bright lights,
Christmas smells like sweets, chocolate, cookies and crunchy carrots cooking in the kitchen.

Nikhil Mandla (6)
Thorpe House Pre-Prep School, Gerrards Cross

A Kitten Poem

A kitten looks like a furry ball with googly eyes
A kitten smells like fresh plums
A kitten tastes like sweet chicken
A kitten sounds like a miaowing cat purring like a lion
A kitten feels like a fluffy tiger.

Ishaan Singh Ghataura (6)
Thorpe House Pre-Prep School, Gerrards Cross

What senses did you enjoy reading about on these pages? Colour the symbols.

Cats

I hear a miaow
Cats feel soft
Cats are cuddly
Smell of fish
And they taste disgusting.

Rakin Arif Rehan (5)
Thorpe House Pre-Prep School, Gerrards Cross

Sweets

Crunching like a clock
The sweets are bumpy
I see the sugar
Mint and fruit
Sugary and delicious.

Shaan Ryatt
Thorpe House Pre-Prep School, Gerrards Cross

What senses did you enjoy reading about on these pages? Colour the symbols.

Ice Lolly

I hear it crunch
It feels cold
I see cold pinkness
It smells delicious
It tastes cold and sweet.

Logan Shields (6)
Thorpe House Pre-Prep School, Gerrards Cross

Dogs

Dogs sound like woof
They feel soft
When they run their tongues stick out
Jumping in muddy water, they smell yucky
I would not taste dog.

Charlie Pandit (5)
Thorpe House Pre-Prep School, Gerrards Cross

Chocolate

I hear a crunch when I bite through the bar of chocolate
When I touch it, it feels lumpy
A brown lumpy rock of deliciousness
The smell of Dairy Milk makes my mouth water!
The taste melts in my mouth.

Akhil Vedi (6)
Thorpe House Pre-Prep School, Gerrards Cross

What senses did you enjoy reading about on these pages? Colour the symbols.

Cake

Crumbs falling into my mouth
Muddy icing melts on my fingers
Candles blinking on the top
Chocolate smells good
Blue buttery icing.

Charlie Ciesielski (5)
Thorpe House Pre-Prep School, Gerrards Cross

Cat

Claws scratching as they run
Soft and fresh
They pounce front, backwards, left and right
Cats smell like fish
Cats taste of cat food.

Jeona Singh Kalley (5)
Thorpe House Pre-Prep School, Gerrards Cross

What senses did you enjoy reading about on these pages? Colour the symbols.

When My Friend Came To Tea

We were on the bus,
We heard cars whooshing past us.
We ran down to see the snails,
We saw a snail's shell and a slug.

At my house we touched the toys.
We had chicken and waffles together,
And some sweeties after dinner.

We hid from Lila's mum,
It smelt yucky under my bed.
Lila didn't want to go home.

She went back in her car,
And I waved to her.

Emily Ruth Harrington (5)
Upton-St-Leonard's CE Primary School, Gloucester

Halloween

Halloween sounds like spooky trees creaking.
I touch my witch's costume and have my photo taken.
In the garden I can see chocolate eyeballs hiding in the bushes.
Halloween smells like pumpkins cooking.
Halloween tastes like apple bobbing and water up my nose.

Sienna Goodman (5)
Upton-St-Leonard's CE Primary School, Gloucester

What senses did you enjoy reading about on these pages? Colour the symbols.

My Friend

We went on the bus, with no seat belts.
We heard cars whooshing past us.
I felt excited.
We walked to her house.
We looked in the mud and we saw a shell.
It was an old snail's one.

I went in her house.
We played upstairs with the dragons.
I smelt the food cooking.
We had a tasty tea with mayo sauce,
We had a Dip-Dab and a Chewer.

My mum knocked on the door.
We hid under the bed.
It was dark. I had to go.
We hugged each other.
And then we waved bye-bye.

Lila Rose Dare (5)
Upton-St-Leonard's CE Primary School, Gloucester

What senses did you enjoy reading about on these pages? Colour the symbols.

A New Baby

A new baby sounds sad
Because she cries for her bottle
On her first night at home.

The touch of a new baby's fingers,
They are very tiny,
We stroke a finger when she cries.

She looks pretty and she smiles lovely.
When she was in hospital I smelled her lovely feet
And they still smell lovely now.

My sister has a bottle with milk
And she has some special drops to stop her being sick.

I can hold her when there is a pillow
I can hold her on my shoulder.
I kiss her on her head.

Paige Knight (5)
Upton-St-Leonard's CE Primary School, Gloucester

What senses did you enjoy reading about on these pages? Colour the symbols.

Nana And Grampy

Grampy tells me stories,
He makes them up,
About my sister and me,
But only on Thursdays when he takes me to school.

When I go to their house,
I touch Thunderbird 2 and Thunderbird 4,
I play with Tracy Island.

My nana cooks every type of cake
They taste really good.
My nana smells like flowers.

My grampy wears a hat
And he's not got much hair in the middle,
And he has a white beard.

Dylan Joseph Cadman (5)
Upton-St-Leonard's CE Primary School, Gloucester

What senses did you enjoy reading about on these pages? Colour the symbols.

My Little Brother

I can hear Harry's happy laughter
As he runs around the house
And bumps down the stairs.

We share tasty sweets in the car,
When we go on holiday.
When he has a bath he comes out smelling lovely.

I touch his soft hair when he is asleep,
But he doesn't normally let me.
When he is asleep he looks really cute.

Rebecca Brotherton (6)
Upton-St-Leonard's CE Primary School, Gloucester

Autumn

What can you smell?
I can smell the cold wind
What can you taste?
I can taste hot soup
What can you feel?
I can feel the wind on my face
What can you hear?
I can hear the wind whistling.

Anikith Kapoor
Wildmoor Heath School, Crowthorne

What senses did you enjoy reading about on these pages? Colour the symbols.

Autumn

What can you smell?
I can smell the breezy air
What can you taste?
I can taste sweet strawberries
What can you hear?
I can hear noisy machines
What can you see?
I can see dirty rubbish
What can you feel?
I can feel crunchy leaves.

Dylan Brinkman
Wildmoor Heath School, Crowthorne

Autumn

What can you smell?
I can smell the chilly autumn breeze
What can you taste?
I can taste ripe strawberries
What can you hear?
I can hear the trees whistling
What can you see?
I can see the trees blowing
What can you feel?
I can feel the green leaves on the trees.

William Brandist
Wildmoor Heath School, Crowthorne

What senses did you enjoy reading about on these pages? Colour the symbols.

Autumn

What can you smell?
I can smell the wind blowing
What can you hear?
I can hear the bushes moving around
What can you see?
I can see the bird's nest up in the tree
What can you feel?
I can feel red leaves on the floor.

Charles Rolls
Wildmoor Heath School, Crowthorne

Autumn

What can you smell, what can you smell?
I can smell leaves whistling on the trees
What can you taste, what can you taste?
I can taste cold air
What can you hear, what can you hear?
Blue cars brooming on the road
What can you see, what can you see?
Branches rustling
What can you feel, what can you feel?
I can feel cold grass on the field.

Lucia Mackie
Wildmoor Heath School, Crowthorne

What senses did you enjoy reading about on these pages? Colour the symbols.

Autumn

What can you smell?
I can smell sweet strawberries
What can you taste?
I can taste the freezing cold air
What can you hear?
I can hear the rain
What can you see?
I can see red leaves
What can you feel?
I can feel pine cones.

Fern Gaunt
Wildmoor Heath School, Crowthorne

Autumn

What can you smell?
I can smell sweet, red strawberries
What can you taste?
I can taste the freezing cold
What can you hear?
I can hear trees swaying side to side
What can you see?
I can see golden leaves
What can you feel?
I can feel the wet grass.

Carol Huynh
Wildmoor Heath School, Crowthorne

What senses did you enjoy reading about on these pages? Colour the symbols.

Autumn

What can you smell?
I can smell golden leaves
What can you taste?
I can taste the whistling wind
What can you hear?
I can hear falling acorns
What can you see?
I can see brown wood
What can you feel?
I can feel the rustling leaves on the trees.

Thomas Bridges
Wildmoor Heath School, Crowthorne

Autumn

What can you smell?
I can smell the damp air
What can you taste?
I can taste crunchy apples
What can you hear?
I can hear the leaves rustling in the trees
What can you see?
I can see birds having a race
What can you feel?
I can feel wet grass.

Luke Gray (5)
Wildmoor Heath School, Crowthorne

What senses did you enjoy reading about on these pages? Colour the symbols.

Untitled

What can you smell?
I can smell the wind
What can you taste?
I can taste acorns, green
What can you hear?
I can hear yellow leaves
What can you see?
I can see red leaves
What can you feel?
I can feel the red blowing wind and conkers.

Emily Castle
Wildmoor Heath School, Crowthorne

Autumn

What can you smell?
I can smell the wet grass on the floor
What can you taste?
I can taste fat blackberries
What can you hear?
I can hear a kitten following me
What can you see?
I can see golden leaves
What can you feel?
I can feel wet grass on my feet.

Kaitlyn Caroline Parsons (6)
Wildmoor Heath School, Crowthorne

What senses did you enjoy reading about on these pages? Colour the symbols.

Autumn

What can you smell?
I can smell the wind and wood
What can you taste?
I can taste the cold wind
What can you see?
I can see the green trees
What can you feel?
I can feel wood
What can you hear?
I can hear the magic wind.

Jodie Ferguson
Wildmoor Heath School, Crowthorne

Autumn

What can you smell?
I can smell the windy trees
What can you taste?
I can taste the juicy blackberries
What can you hear?
I can hear the trees blowing
What can you see?
I can see the conkers falling off. The bush is blowing
What can you smell?
I can smell the trees and the breeze whistling
What can you feel?
I can feel the muddy mud.

Sadie Ellis (5)
Wildmoor Heath School, Crowthorne

What senses did you enjoy reading about on these pages? Colour the symbols.

III

Autumn

What can you smell?
I can smell the green scarecrow
What can you see?
I can see the tree blowing in the wind
What can you feel?
I can feel conkers
What can you hear?
I can hear whistling trees.

Theo Foster
Wildmoor Heath School, Crowthorne

Autumn

What can you smell?
I can smell the wet, brown acorns
What can you taste?
I can taste wind
What can you hear?
I can hear the trees
What can you see?
I can see the birds
What can you feel?
I can feel acorns.

Daniel Furzer
Wildmoor Heath School, Crowthorne

What senses did you enjoy reading about on these pages? Colour the symbols.

Autumn

What can you smell?
I can smell the air
What can you see?
I can see the clouds moving
What can you hear?
I can hear the wind
What can you feel?
I can feel the leaves
What can you taste?
I can taste the cheese.

Daniel Scott
Wildmoor Heath School, Crowthorne

Autumn

What can you smell, what can you smell?
I can smell the wind tumbling
What can you taste, what can you taste?
I can taste the windy wind
What can you see, what can you see?
I can see the birds in the cold sky
What can you hear, what can you hear?
I can hear the whistling wind
What can you feel, what can you feel?
I can feel acorns that have fallen on the ground.

Mykaela Cairo
Wildmoor Heath School, Crowthorne

What senses did you enjoy reading about on these pages? Colour the symbols.

Christmas

Christmas tastes like yummy treats
Christmas feels soft, like soft big pillows
Christmas sounds like dancing reindeer
Christmas looks like you are in heaven
Christmas smells like foggy air.

Yasmin Lucia Albert (6)
Wildmoor Heath School, Crowthorne

Alligator

Green like grass, they blend into their surroundings
Alligators are as hard as rock, with spikes on the top
Alligators are silent and quiet and relaxing in the swamp
Tastes like wet, damp grass or something like grass
Alligators smell like grass or something like wet, damp grass.

Yariv Gelbolingo
Wildmoor Heath School, Crowthorne

Chocolate

Chocolate smells like ice cream and milk
Chocolate tastes like milk
Chocolate looks like sauce
Chocolate feels like smooth hands
Chocolate sounds like melting.

Isabelle Steel (7)
Wildmoor Heath School, Crowthorne

What senses did you enjoy reading about on these pages? Colour the symbols.

Halloween

Halloween smells like sweet pumpkins
Throwing big seeds at you
Halloween tastes like lots of fresh sweets coming into your mouth
Halloween sounds like people saying, 'Trick or treat?'

Patrick Resurreccion
Wildmoor Heath School, Crowthorne

Halloween

Halloween tastes like old, mouldy sweets
On Halloween you could touch candy
At Halloween you see wicked witches
Halloween sounds like people going around getting sweets
Halloween smells like mouldy wood.

Anton Nawala
Wildmoor Heath School, Crowthorne

Christmas

Christmas smells like the cold winter air
Christmas tastes like icy drinks
Christmas sounds like cheerful laughter.

Cloe Ysabel Powell (6)
Wildmoor Heath School, Crowthorne

What senses did you enjoy reading about on these pages? Colour the symbols.

Chocolate

Chocolate smells like creamy custard
Chocolate tastes like creamy milk
Chocolate sounds like crunching leaves
Chocolate feels like a freezing ice cube
Chocolate looks like a brown tree as brown as mud.

Miles Miller (6)
Wildmoor Heath School, Crowthorne

Summer Chocolate

I can taste chocolate crunch and crumbs
The chocolate is smooth
Chocolate looks like mud
Chocolate smells like fresh daffodils
Chocolate sounds like a crunch.

Bethany Farns
Wildmoor Heath School, Crowthorne

Christmas

Christmas smells like lovely crunchy cookies
I can see the dropping snow from the sky and people building snowmen
And people sitting inside near the fire
I can hear people laughing in the snow
I can taste the crushing cookies.

Nicole Christina Bennett (6)
Wildmoor Heath School, Crowthorne

What senses did you enjoy reading about on these pages? Colour the symbols.

Chocolate

I can hear chocolate going crunch, crunch in my gooey mouth.
I can taste the chocolate melting in my gooey mouth.
I can smell the hot chocolate melting in the hot pan.
I can feel the bumps on the chocolate.
When I see chocolate I can't resist a piece.

Olivia Robson
Wildmoor Heath School, Crowthorne

Halloween

Halloween smells like horrible witches because of the dark, dark night
Halloween feels like I'm feeling sweets that make me sleepy and crazy
I can hear children screaming loudly all night
I can taste strawberry sweets that are really nice.

Josh Cooper (6)
Wildmoor Heath School, Crowthorne

Cake

The cake looks so yummy and tasty, yum-yum
I really just want it in my tummy
Cake tastes so creamy and crumbly and curly, mmm
Cake feels all squishy and scrummy, ooh lala.

Logie Barr
Wildmoor Heath School, Crowthorne

What senses did you enjoy reading about on these pages? Colour the symbols.

Untitled

Fireworks exploding, a rainbow of colourful patterns
Sizzling sausages by the fire
Sticky, toasted marshmallows
Children happy and laughing
Snap, crackle, pop.

Summer-Rose Hawkins (6)
Woodfield Primary School, Plymouth

Untitled

Bonfire Night smells like burning hot smoke
Bonfire Night tastes like smoky bacon burgers
Bonfire Night looks like sparkling colours, popping up in the blue sky
Bonfire Night feels cold outside and warm inside
Bonfire Night sounds loud and like *crash, boom, boom*
I like Bonfire Night, it's fun
Then *pop*, children screaming, babies crying, sausages sizzling and
fireworks banging.

Tiffany Lake (7)
Woodfield Primary School, Plymouth

What senses did you enjoy reading about on these pages? Colour the symbols.

Bonfire Night

Bonfire Night smells like smoky marshmallows and tasty hot chocolate
Bonfire Night tastes like sweet toffee apples and burning fiery flames
Bonfire Night looks sparkly and nice like a colourful bright rainbow
Bonfire Night feels dark and damp and black as soot and a bright orange fire
Bonfire Night feels like *bang, boom, pop, crackle* and *crash.*

Freya Roberts (6)
Woodfield Primary School, Plymouth

Untitled

Bonfire Night smells just like toasting marshmallows and bacon and it smells smoky
Bonfire Night tastes like sizzling sausages and gooey marshmallows
Bonfire Night looks so sparkly, I see sparkles, sparkling in the dark
Bonfire Night feels so great, I would have it every day
Bonfire Night sounds so loud, my ears go *pop, pop, pop* and the sausages go *crackle, crackle.*

Ella Simpson (6)
Woodfield Primary School, Plymouth

What senses did you enjoy reading about on these pages? Colour the symbols.

Young Writers
Information

We hope you have enjoyed reading this book – and that you will continue to in the coming years.

If you're a young writer who enjoys reading and creative writing, or the parent of an enthusiastic poet or story writer, do visit our website **www.youngwriters.co.uk**. Here you will find free competitions, workshops and games, as well as recommended reads, a poetry glossary and our blog.

If you would like to order further copies of this book, or any of our other titles give us a call or visit **www.youngwriters.co.uk**.

Young Writers
Remus House
Coltsfoot Drive
Peterborough
PE2 9BF

(01733) 890066
info@youngwriters.co.uk

Share your feelings verse any time!